Happy Bithd[...]

We hope this coming
year will be a very
special celibration filled
with lots of dancing,
clapping and days
filled with laughter!

Fondly,
Peter, his mom,
his dad and
his brother
R.D.!!

6/25/94

CHARLOTTE AGELL

Dancing Feet

GULLIVER BOOKS

HARCOURT BRACE & COMPANY

San Diego   New York   London

Library of Congress Cataloging-in-Publication Data
Agell, Charlotte.
Dancing feet/Charlotte Agell. — 1st ed.
p.   cm.
"Gulliver books."
Summary: Rhyming text and illustrations celebrate
the diversity of the world's cultures.
ISBN 0-15-200444-0
[1. Manners and customs — Fiction. 2. Stories in rhyme.]
I. Title.
PZ8.3.A2595Dan   1994
[E] — dc20   93-17251

Printed in Singapore

First edition
A B C D E

The paintings in this book were done in Winsor & Newton watercolors, Berol
Prismacolor Stix, and India Ink on Arches hot-press watercolor paper.
The display type was set in Bolide Script by the Photocomposition Center,
Harcourt Brace & Company, San Diego, California.
The text type was set in Berling by Thompson Type, San Diego, California.
Color separations by Bright Arts, Ltd., Singapore
Printed and bound by Tien Wah Press, Singapore
Production supervision by Warren Wallerstein and Ginger Boyer
Designed by Lori J. McThomas

for Peter, Anna, and Jon

Feet, feet

walking down the street,

dancing on the earth,

skipping to the beat.

Hands, hands

digging in the sand,

baking homemade bread,

playing in the band.

Hair, hair

waving in the air,

shining when it's wet,

getting special care.

Arms, arms

pulling with strong tugs,

holding heavy tools,

giving hearty hugs.

Legs, legs

strolling through the town.

Eyes, eyes

looking left and right,

crying tears sometimes,

resting through the night.

Mouths, mouths

sipping on a drink,

tasting something new,

saying what they think.

People young and old

doing what they do,

living in the world,

and one of them is you!